Date Due

	MAY 13 '99	
NOV 2 0 '99	MAR 18 00	MAY 12 '04
DEC 05 '99	APR 11 00	SEP 27 05
DEC 1 4 '99	MAY 02 00	
JAN 2 0 '99		
FEB 1 6 '99	JUL 05 00	
MAR 1 0 '99	SEP 11 00	
APR 02 '99	JUN 10 01	
APR 23 '99	FEB 03 01	

THE
CRYSTAL
HEART

T·H·E CRYSTAL

HEART

✦⧜ A Vietnamese Legend ⧜✦

retold by AARON SHEPARD

illustrated by JOSEPH DANIEL FIEDLER

FOR YOUNG READERS

HOW TO SAY THE NAMES

Mi Nuong   MEE NWONG
Truong Chi   troo-ONG CHEE

Atheneum Books for Young Readers
An imprint of Simon & Schuster Children's Publishing Division
1230 Avenue of the Americas
New York, New York 10020

Book design by Nina Barnett

The text of this book is set in Venetian.
The illustrations are rendered in Winsor & Newton alkyd.

First Edition
Printed in Hong Kong
10 9 8 7 6 5 4 3 2 1
Library of Congress Cataloging-in-Publication Data
Shepard, Aaron.
The crystal heart : a Vietnamese legend / retold by Aaron Shepard :
illustrated by Joseph Daniel Fiedler.
p. cm.
Summary: The sheltered and privileged daughter of a mandarin comes to
understand the consequences of her naive, yet cruel, words to a fisherman.
ISBN 0-689-81551-4
[1. Folklore—Vietnam.] I. Fiedler, Joseph Daniel, ill. II. Title.
PZ8.1.S53945Cr   1998
398.209597'02—dc21
[E] 97-3016
CIP   AC

For Barbara Kouts
—A. S.

For Anne Steytler
—J. D. F.

Long ago, in a palace by the Red River, there lived a great mandarin and his daughter, Mi Nuong.

Like other young ladies of her position, Mi Nuong was kept indoors, away from the eyes of admiring men. She spent most of her time in her room at the top of a tower. There she would sit on a bench by a moon-shaped window, reading or embroidering, chatting with her maid, and gazing out often at the garden and the river.

One day as she sat there, a song floated to her from the distance, in a voice deep and sweet. She looked out and saw a fishing boat coming up the river.

"Do you hear it?" she asked her maid. "How beautifully he sings!" She listened again as the voice drew nearer.

My love is like a blossom in the breeze.
My love is like a moonbeam on the waves.

"He must be young and very handsome," said Mi Nuong. She felt a sudden thrill. "Perhaps he knows I am here and sings it just for me!"

The maid's eyes lit up. "My lady, perhaps he's a mandarin's son in disguise—the man you are destined to marry!"

Mi Nuong felt a flush on her face and a stirring in her heart. She tried to make out the man's features, but he was too far off to see clearly. The boat and the song glided slowly up the river and away.

"Yes," she said softly. "Perhaps he is."

All day long, Mi Nuong waited by the window, hoping to hear the singer again. The next day she waited too, and the next. But the voice did not return.

"Why doesn't he come?" she asked her maid sadly.

As the days passed, Mi Nuong grew pale and weak. At last she went to her bed and stayed there.

The mandarin came to her. "Daughter, what's wrong?"

"It's nothing, Father," she said faintly.

The mandarin sent for the doctor. But after seeing Mi Nuong, the doctor told him, "I can find no illness. And without an illness, I can offer no cure."

The weeks passed, and Mi Nuong grew no
better. Then one day her maid came before the
mandarin.

"My lord, I know what ails your daughter. Mi
Nuong is sick for love. To cure her, you must find
the handsome young man who sings this song."
And she sang it for him.

"It will be done," said the mandarin, and he sent
out a messenger at once.

Days later, the messenger returned.

"Lord, in no great house of this province does any young man know the song. But in a nearby village I found a man who sings it, a fisherman named Truong Chi. I have brought him to the palace."

"A fisherman?" said the mandarin in disbelief. "Let me see him."

The messenger brought him in. The fisherman stood uneasily, his eyes wide as they cast about the richly furnished room.

For a moment, the mandarin was too astounded to speak. The man was neither young nor handsome. His clothes were ragged and he stank of fish. *Certainly no match for my daughter!* thought the mandarin. *Somehow, she must not realize . . .*

He gave his order to the messenger. "Bring the fisherman to my daughter's door and have him sing his song."

Soon Truong Chi stood anxiously outside the young lady's room. He could not understand why they'd brought him here. What could they want? He was just a fisherman, wishing only to make an honest living. He had hurt no one, done nothing wrong!

At the messenger's signal, he nervously started to sing.

My love is like a blossom in the breeze.
My love is like a moonbeam on the waves.

In the room beyond the door, Mi Nuong's eyes flew open. "He's here!" she cried to her maid. "How can that be? Oh, quickly, help me dress!"

Mi Nuong jumped from her bed. Never had she so swiftly clothed herself, put up her hair, made herself up. By the time the song drew to a close, she looked like a heavenly vision in flowing robes.

"Now, open the door!" she said, trying to calm her wildly beating heart. She forced herself to stand shyly, casting her eyes down in the manner proper to a modest young lady.

As the door pulled open, Truong Chi shrank back, not knowing what to expect. Then all at once he found himself gazing on the greatest beauty he had ever known. He felt his heart leap, and in that moment, he fell deeply, hopelessly, desperately in love.

Mi Nuong could not wait a moment longer. She lifted her eyes to look upon her beloved. And in that moment, her eyes grew wide and she burst out laughing.

A mandarin's son? Her destined love? Why, he was nothing but a common fisherman! How terribly, terribly silly she'd been!

Shaking with mirth at her folly, she turned her head away and whispered, "Close the door."

The door shut in Truong Chi's face. He stood there frozen, the young lady's laughter ringing in his ears. He felt his heart grow cold and hard.

Truong Chi was sent home. But he could not go on as before. Hardly eating or sleeping, he grew pale and ill. He no longer cared if he lived or died.

And so he died.

The villagers found him on the sleeping mat in his hut. On his chest sat a large crystal.

"What is it?" a man asked.

"It is his heart," said a wise old woman. "The laugh of the mandarin's daughter wounded it so deeply, it turned hard to stop the pain."

"What do we do with it?" asked a young woman. "It is very lovely. Like one of his songs!"

"We should put it in his boat," said another young man, "and let it float down to the sea."

At sundown, they set the crystal in the fisherman's boat. Then they pushed the boat from its mooring and watched in sorrow as it drifted down the river and out of sight.

But the boat did not drift to the sea. It came to shore by the mandarin's palace. And so it was that the mandarin found it at sunrise as he strolled along the bank.

"What have we here?" he said, reaching in to pick up the crystal. He turned it over in his hand, examining and admiring it. "What a splendid gift the river has brought!"

A few days later, when no one had claimed it, the
mandarin sent it to a turner to be made into a teacup.
He brought the cup one evening to Mi Nuong's room.
   "A gift for my lovely daughter," he said.
   "Oh, Father, it's beautiful!
I can hardly wait to drink
from it!"
   When the mandarin
left, she told her
maid, "It's late,
so you can go to
bed. But first
make me some
tea, so I can
drink from
my cup."

The maid fin-
ished her task and went
off. Mi Nuong poured the
tea, blew out the candles on the
table, and carried the cup to her
window seat. A full moon shone
into the room, and looking out,
she watched the moonlight play
upon the river. The scent of
blossoms drifted from
the garden.

Mi Nuong lifted the cup to her lips. But just as she was about to drink, she cried out in surprise and fear. She quickly set the cup down on the bench.

On the surface of the tea was the face of Truong Chi, gazing at her with eyes filled with love. And now his sweet song filled the room, familiar but a little changed.

Mi Nuong is like a blossom in the breeze.
Mi Nuong is like a moonbeam on the waves.

And Mi Nuong remembered those eyes she had seen so briefly through the open door, and she remembered her laugh.

"What have I done? I was so cruel! I didn't mean to hurt you. I didn't know . . . I'm sorry. So very, very sorry!"

Her eyes filled with tears. A single tear dropped into the cup.

It was enough. The crystal melted away, releasing the spirit of Truong Chi. Then Mi Nuong heard the song one last time, floating off over the river.

Mi Nuong is like a blossom in the breeze.
Mi Nuong is like a moonbeam on the waves.

"Good-bye," said Mi Nuong softly. "Good-bye."

It was not many months more when Mi Nuong was given in marriage to the son of a great mandarin. He was young and handsome, and she felt that her dreams had come true.

Yet now, as she gazed on a different garden and a different view of the river, she often still heard the song of the fisherman echo softly in her heart.

THE SONG OF THE FISHERMAN

Words and music by Aaron Shepard

My love is like a blos-som in the breeze. My love is like a moon-beam on the waves.

The melody and words of this song are my own, composed for this retelling. The distinctive flavor comes from the pentatonic (five-note) scale, common to most East Asian traditional music.

ABOUT THE STORY

For the retelling of this popular Vietnamese legend, numerous versions were consulted, the most important being "Le Cristal D'Amour" in *Légendes des Terres Sereines* by Pham Duy Khiêm (Paris: Mercure de France, 1951) and "Truong-Chi and Mi-Nuong" in *Vietnamese Legends* by L. T. Bach-Lan (Saigon: private printing, 1957).

For a reader's theater script of this story and a recording of "The Song of the Fisherman", visit my home page on the World Wide Web at www.aaronshep.com.

AARON SHEPARD